A Note to Parents and Caregivers:

Read-it! Joke Books are for children who are moving ahead on the amazing road to reading. These fun books support the acquisition and extension of reading skills as well as a love of books.

Published by the same company that produces *Read-it!* Readers, these books introduce the question/answer pattern that helps children expand their thinking about language structure and book formats.

When sharing a book with your child, read in short stretches, pausing often to talk about the pictures and the meaning of the book. The question/answer format works well for this purpose and provides an opportunity to talk about the language and meaning of the jokes. Have your child turn the pages and point to the pictures and familiar words. Read the story in a natural voice; have fun creating the voices of characters or emphasizing some important words. And be sure to re-read favorite parts.

There is no right or wrong way to share books with children. Find time to read with your child and pass on the legacy of literacy.

Adria F. Klein, Ph.D.
Professor Emeritus
California State University
San Bernardino, California

Editor: Nadia Higgins
Designer: John Moldstad
Page production: Picture Window Books
The illustrations in this book were prepared digitally.

Picture Window Books
5115 Excelsior Boulevard
Suite 232
Minneapolis, MN 55416
1-877-845-8392
www.picturewindowbooks.com

Printed in the United States of America.
1 2 3 4 5 6 08 07 06 05 04 03

Library of Congress Cataloging-in-Publication Data
Dahl, Michael.
School buzz : classy and funny jokes about school /
written by Michael Dahl ; illustrated by Jeff Yesh.
p. cm.
Summary: A collection of easy-to-read jokes and riddles about school.
ISBN 1-4048-0121-9 (library binding)
1. Schools—Juvenile humor. 2. Education—Juvenile humor.
[1. Schools—Humor. 2. Jokes. 3. Riddles.]
I. Yesh, Jeff, 1971– ill. II. Title.
PN6231.S3 D34 2003
818'.602—dc21

2002156339

School
Buzz
Classy and Funny Jokes About School

Michael Dahl • Illustrated by Jeff Yesh

Reading Advisers:
Adria F. Klein, Ph.D.
Professsor Emeritus, California State University
San Bernardino, California

Susan Kesselring, M.A., Literacy Educator
Rosemount-Apple Valley-Eagan (Minnesota) School District

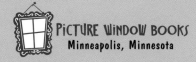

PICTURE WINDOW BOOKS
Minneapolis, Minnesota

1399 8430

How do bees get to school?

By school buzz.

What did one math book say to the other math book?

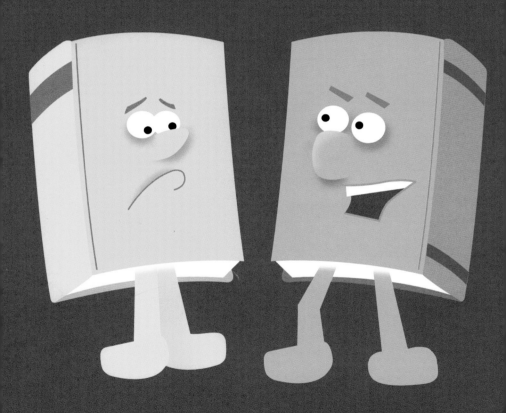

"Boy, do I have problems!"

Why did the student keep a flashlight in his lunch box?

It was a light lunch.

Parent: Would you like a pocket calculator for school?

Child: I already know
how many pockets I have.

What kind of snack does the computer teacher like?

Microchips.

School nurse: Have your eyes ever been checked?

Student: No, they've
always been blue.

What did the sloppy student get on his math test?

Peanut butter and jelly.

Why did the science teacher take a ruler to bed?

She wanted to see
how long she slept.

What do you call a basketball player's pet chicken?

A personal fowl.

Why did the cross-eyed teacher quit her job?

She couldn't control her pupils.   15

Science teacher: What is a light year?

Student: A year
with very little homework.

Why did the teacher wear sunglasses?

Because his class was so bright.

How did the teacher keep his new students on their toes?

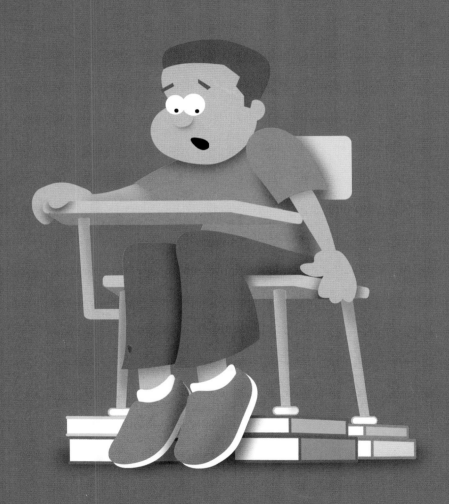

He raised all the chairs.

Why is six afraid of seven?

Because seven ate nine.

What did zero say to the number eight?

"Nice belt."

Teacher: If I had seven oranges in one hand and eight oranges in the other, what would I have?

Student: Big hands!

Why did Cinderella's team lose the volleyball game?

Because their coach was a pumpkin.